Dinner T[i...]
for Bella and Rosie

BY MICHÈLE DUFRESNE

Pioneer Valley Educational Press, Inc.

We like to eat hamburgers.

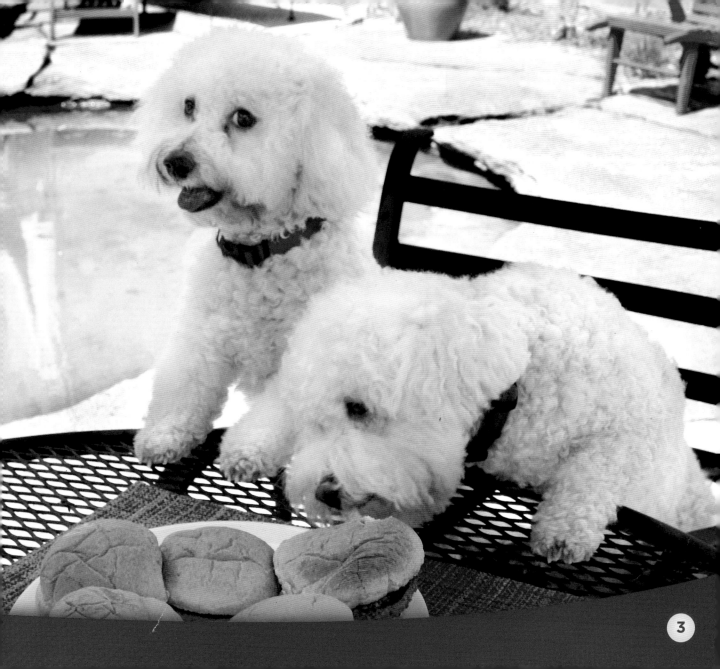

We like to eat hot dogs.

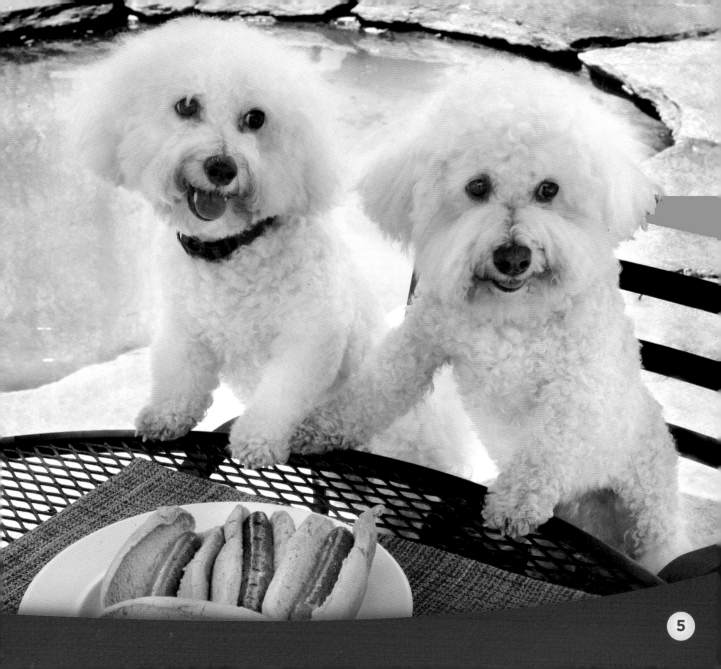

We like to eat corn.

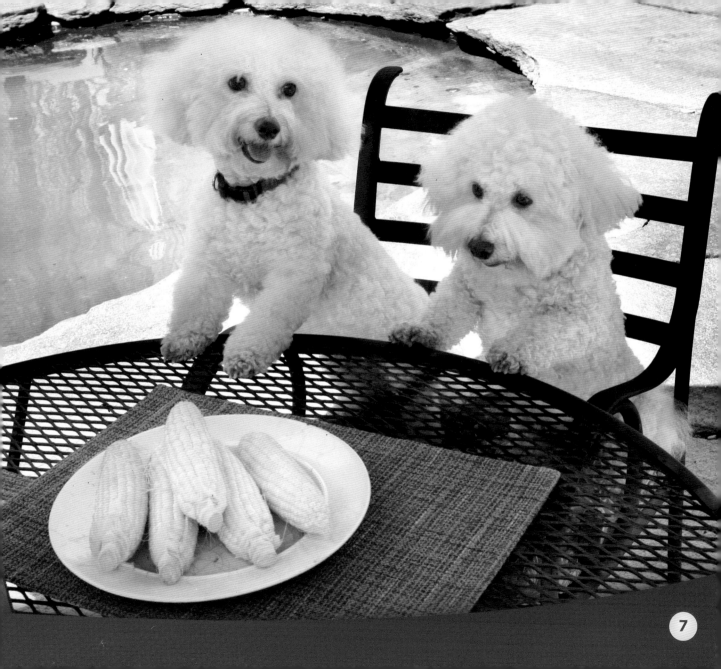

We like to eat salad.

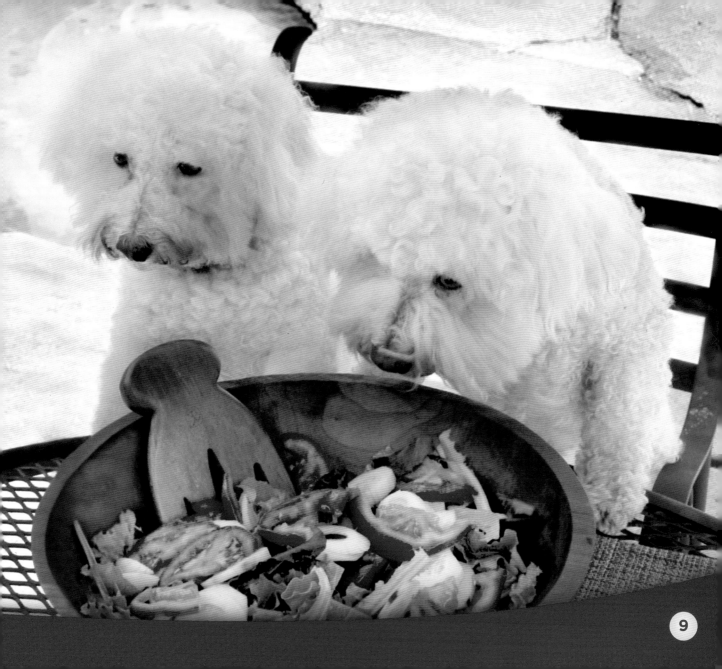

We like to eat pie.

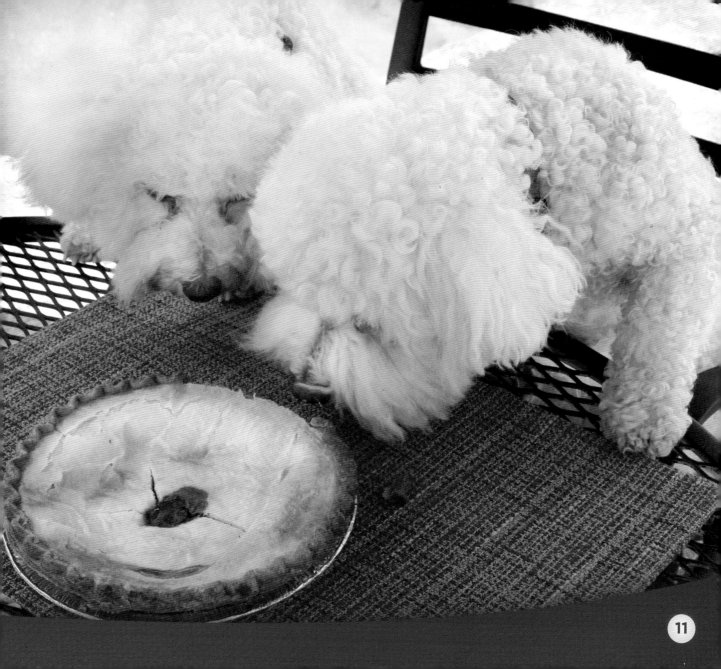

We **love** to eat bones.

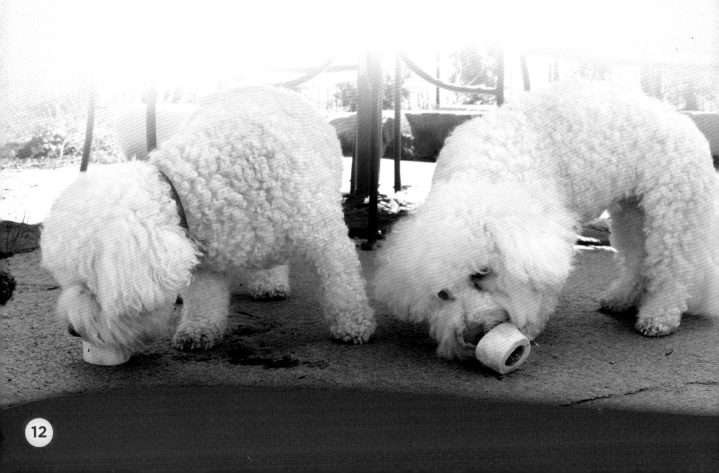